Look the mess!

Katie Carr

National Literacy Strategy

Encourage your child to recognize these essential words
as you read this story:

and   at   door   get   go   his   look
mum   on   said   the   then

"Shut the door, Mike!" said his Mum.

"Look at all the mess!" she said.

"Go and get the mop," said Mum.

Mike got the mop.

Then Mum's mug fell on the mat!

"Look at the mess!" said Mike.

"Get the mop, Mike!" said Mum.

Pups in the pond

Katie Carr

National Literacy Strategy
Encourage your child to recognize these essential words
as you read this story:

a   am   and   are   it   jump   play   see
the   then   they   to   up   we   with

"It's hot," says Peter.

Then Peter sees a pup.

Peter plays with the pup.

They run and jump.

They puff and pant.

They plod up to the pond.

Jump! Splash!

Yes, Granny

Katie Carr

National Literacy Strategy
Encourage your child to recognize these essential words
as you read this story:

a   away   day   for   girl   going   got
had   have   I   is   my   no   not
said   the   yes   you

Granny is going away for the day.

"Have I got my ticket?" said Granny.

"Yes, Granny," said Golden Girl.

"Have I got my bag?" said Granny.

"Yes, Granny," said Golden Girl.

"Have I had a hug?" said Granny.

"No, you have not!" said Golden Girl.

Sorry, Sammy

Katie Carr

National Literacy Strategy
Encourage your child to recognize these essential words
as you read this story:

a   and   by   day   for   it   on   said
the   very   was   went

It was a very hot day.

Eddy Elephant slept on the sand.

Sammy and Ben went by.

"Sorry, Eddy," said Sammy.

Eddy and Sammy went for a swim.

Splish! Splash! Splosh!

"Sorry, Sammy!" said Eddy.